Magic Ponies

A Twinkle of Hooves

To Hoppy, and first-ever lessons—SB

GROSSET & DUNLAP
Published by the Penguin Group
Penguin Group (USA) Inc., 375 Hudson Street, New York, New York 10014, USA
Penguin Group (Canada), 90 Eglinton Avenue East, Suite 700, Toronto, Ontario M4P 2Y3, Canada
(a division of Pearson Penguin Canada Inc.)
Penguin Books Ltd, 80 Strand, London WC2R 0RL, England
Penguin Ireland, 25 St Stephen's Green, Dublin 2, Ireland (a division of Penguin Books Ltd)
Penguin Group (Australia), 707 Collins Street, Melbourne, Victoria 3008, Australia
(a division of Pearson Australia Group Pty Ltd)
Penguin Books India Pvt Ltd, 11 Community Centre, Panchsheel Park, New Delhi—110 017,
India Penguin Group (NZ), 67 Apollo Drive, Rosedale, Auckland 0632, New Zealand
(a division of Pearson New Zealand Ltd)
Penguin Books (South Africa), Rosebank Office Park, 181 Jan Smuts Avenue,
Parktown North 2193, South Africa
Penguin China, B7 Jiaming Center, 27 East Third Ring Road North,
Chaoyang District, Beijing 100020, China

Penguin Books Ltd, Registered Offices: 80 Strand, London WC2R 0RL, England

Text copyright © 2009 by Sue Bentley. Illustrations copyright © 2009 by Angela Swan. Cover illustration © 2009 by Andrew Farley. First printed in Great Britain in 2009 by Penguin Books Ltd. First published in the United States in 2013 by Grosset & Dunlap, a division of Penguin Young Readers Group, 345 Hudson Street, New York, New York 10014. GROSSET & DUNLAP is a trademark of Penguin Group (USA) Inc. Printed in the U.S.A.

Library of Congress Cataloging-in-Publication Data is available.

ISBN 978-0-448-46207-3   10 9 8 7 6 5 4 3 2

ALWAYS LEARNING   PEARSON

Magic Ponies

A Twinkle of Hooves

SUE BENTLEY

illustrated by Angela Swan

Grosset & Dunlap
An Imprint of Penguin Group (USA) Inc.

Prologue

Comet folded his gold-feathered wings as his hooves touched down on the grass of his magical island home. The magic pony felt excited. Surely his twin sister was here, safely among the Lightning Herd once again.

"I can't wait to see Destiny! She has been lost for so long," Comet cried, his violet eyes flashing.

It was a hot day and he was thirsty. Trotting toward a crystal stream, he drank deeply. Sunlight, filtering through a nearby birch tree, gleamed on his cream coat and flowing golden mane and tail.

Lifting his head, he peered through the woods on the far side of the stream. Beyond them the magic pony could see gently rolling hills and the tops of the snow-capped mountains, wreathed in the softly shimmering, multicolored clouds that gave Rainbow Mist Island its name.

Suddenly, the trees swayed as a shadowy shape moved through them. Comet twitched his ears forward eagerly.

"Destiny?"

There was no answer. Puzzled, he took a step and then stopped in alarm. Perhaps it was one of the dark horses, waiting in ambush! They were always plotting to steal the Lightning Horses' magic.

Tremors flickered over Comet's silky coat and he flexed his magnificent golden wings, ready to soar away to safety.

An older cream-and-gold horse with a wise expression and glowing dark eyes stepped out of the trees and splashed across the stream toward him.

"Blaze!" Comet cried in relief. He bent his head in greeting before the leader of the Lightning Herd.

Blaze's eyes softened with affection. "I am glad to see you again, my young friend. Have you brought Destiny back with you?" he asked in a deep, velvety neigh.

"No. I was hoping that she had returned by herself," Comet told him sadly.

"But I see now that I was mistaken."

Blaze looked at him gravely. "I do not think Destiny will ever come back, unless you find her and explain that the stone has been found."

The Stone of Power protected the Lightning Herd from the evil dark horses. Destiny had accidentally lost it during a game of cloud-racing with Comet. Comet found the stone, but Destiny had already fled in panic, thinking she was in a lot of trouble.

"I must look for her again," Comet decided. "She is in danger from the dark horses!"

Blaze pawed at the ground with one shining hoof. There was a flash of rainbow light and a beautiful fiery opal appeared.

"Come closer, Comet. Look into the stone," Blaze neighed.

The magic pony moved nearer to the Stone of Power. He felt warm tingles move over his body as the stone grew larger and rays of dazzling rainbow light spread out from it. Comet gasped as he saw an image of Destiny form, galloping along a track beside redbrick houses, in a world far away.

There was a bright flash of violet light and suddenly a rainbow mist surrounded Comet. The young cream pony with his flowing golden mane and powerful gleaming gold wings disappeared. In his place stood a small black-and-white pony with a broad white stripe down his black face.

"Use this disguise to protect yourself

as you go into the other world. Go now, my young friend," urged Blaze.

"I will find Destiny and bring her back!" Comet vowed.

The pony's black-and-white coat bloomed with violet sparks and a rainbow mist surrounded him. Comet neighed softly as he felt the power building inside him. The shimmering mist swirled faster and faster as it drew him in . . .

Chapter ONE

"Bye, Alice! I hope you and Fleur
will be really happy!" Steph Danes called,
her voice catching. She waved to the six-
year-old girl who sat in the front seat of
the car parked outside her house.

"Thank you. We will!" The little girl
waved back, her small face shining with
happiness.

Steph's eyes pricked with tears as the

car and the horse trailer it was towing
moved slowly away up Porlock Close. She
watched until they were out of sight and
then her face crumpled as she turned to
her mom.

Mrs. Danes gave her daughter a hug
and stroked her short fair hair. "Good job,

honey. I know it was hard for you to let Fleur go. But we don't have the room to keep a pony you won't be riding anymore."

"I know." Steph sighed, wiping her eyes. "And Fleur's going to a good home. Alice really seemed to love her, didn't she?"

Her mom nodded, smiling fondly. "All little girls love their very own first pony the best. You were Alice's age when we got Fleur. It's too bad that you've outgrown her, but it happens to everyone eventually."

Steph nodded. She knew her mom was right, but she was going to miss Fleur, her little chestnut Dartmoor pony, like crazy. They'd had so much fun together in the last three years. Steph was going to feel very lonely not seeing her every day.

Steph and her mom walked back into

the house together. It was hot in the kitchen with the bright sun pouring in through the open back door. Steph got them cold drinks from the fridge.

She stared into space as she drank, feeling sad. Saturdays were usually for riding, and then grooming Fleur until her chestnut coat gleamed.

"Do you want to clear out the stable?" Mrs. Danes asked. "You could practice what you learned at that workshop on stable management over spring break."

Steph had really enjoyed the workshop. She wanted to work with horses when she grew up. "I guess I could do that now," she answered, deciding to get the upsetting task of removing all traces of Fleur over and done with.

Steph went outside to the old garage

at the side of the house. Her dad had converted it into a stable when they'd had the driveway extended and a bigger garage built. As she forked up soiled bedding and began to wheel it away, she felt an overwhelming wave of sadness. Fleur wasn't even here to appreciate what she was doing.

What was Steph going to do now without her very own little pony to look after and love? She sighed heavily before giving the stable floor one last mopping, but as she did a car drove up the cul-de-sac and pulled into the driveway.

Her dad got out and walked around to her. "Hello, sweetie. Keeping busy?" he asked.

Steph nodded. "I'm almost done. It's horrible, though, without Fleur."

"It must be," Mr. Danes agreed sympathetically. "We'll all miss her." He gave her a hug. "I knew you'd need cheering up, so I popped into the new riding stables in the village. Judy Marshall, the owner, says they aren't too busy today. You can go right over and have your pick of the ponies to ride."

Steph stared at him in surprise. How could he even think that she'd want to ride a pony she didn't know? It was far too soon. She'd feel disloyal to Fleur.

"I don't really feel like it right now. Maybe some other time," she murmured.

"I don't like to think of you sitting around brooding," her dad said kindly. "Why don't you give the new stables a try? Riding's what you love doing the most, after all, isn't it?" he asked gently.

"Well, yes—usually," Steph admitted. She still wasn't sure that this was a good idea, but her dad had gone out of his way to get her a ride and she didn't want to hurt his feelings. "I guess I could go over there and take a look."

"That's the spirit! Come on, grab your riding gear. I'll have a quick word with your mom. See you in the car."

Despite herself, Steph felt a bit brighter because of his enthusiasm. Maybe getting to know some new ponies would be fun and help her miss Fleur less—at least for a little while. "Okay." She sighed. "Thanks, Dad."

She went into the house, put on her boots, and came back out holding her riding hat by the chin strap.

"All set!" Mr. Danes started the engine.

It was only a few minutes' drive to
Marshall's Stables. Mr. Danes and Steph
went toward the office just as Judy Marshall
was coming out. She was a slim woman
with dark hair, a round face, and friendly
blue eyes.

"Hi! You must be Steph. Nice to meet
you," she said, smiling.

"Nice to meet you, too, Mrs. Marshall,"

Steph said, making an effort to be polite. She still wasn't sure that she wanted to do this.

"Call me Judy. Everyone does. Come and meet the ponies." She turned to Mr. Danes. "Steph will be fine now. We'll look after her."

"See you later then, sweetie. Have a good time."

"Bye, Dad." Steph watched him walk away and then followed Judy toward the main stable block.

The smart redbrick buildings were around two sides of a square. Two smallish ponies were tied up outside the tack room. A boy and a girl in riding gear stood waiting to mount.

"Judy? Someone's on the phone for you!" a voice called.

"Coming!" Judy answered. She
turned to Steph. "Sorry, but I need to
take this call. Why don't you have a look
around? Just check with a staff member
before you take a pony out, okay?"

Steph nodded, smiling awkwardly.
"Thanks, Judy."

She walked toward the loose boxes.
The ponies turned to look at her,
twitching their ears curiously. Steph
went along the row, stroking and patting
each one in turn. Their names were on
the doors: Jiggy, Binky, Misty, Lady, and
Rags. They were all nice, but none of
them were Fleur. She fondly remembered
the little chestnut pony's silky mane.

At the end of the row, there was an
empty box. As Steph reached it there
was a bright flash and sparkling rainbow

mist filled the walls of the box. Rainbow drops settled on her skin, glittering in the afternoon light.

"Oh!" Steph blinked, trying to see through the strange mist.

As it slowly cleared, she saw that there was in fact a pony in there after all. It was a handsome black-and-white piebald with a broad white stripe down its nose and large deep-violet eyes. How could she

have missed it before? But Steph couldn't deny he was there now and as the pony looked at her inquisitively, Steph felt her heart melt just a little.

"Hello, you!" she crooned gently. She'd never seen a pony with eyes that color. Maybe she could ride him. *But just so I can tell Dad that I did*, Steph thought quickly.

Opening the door, she went inside and lifted her hand to stroke the pony's satiny cheek. It turned to look at her.

"Can you help me, please?" it asked in a velvety neigh.

Chapter
TWO

Steph dropped her hand and looked at the black-and-white pony in complete shock. She must be imagining things. Whoever heard of a pony that could talk?

"I wonder what your name is," she murmured. It wasn't written on the door like all the others.

The pony's eyes glowed brightly as it lifted its head. "I am called Comet. And

I have arrived from Rainbow Mist Island.
What is your name?"

Steph did a double take. She hadn't
imagined it. This pony actually was speaking
to her! His large intelligent eyes gazed at
her and he blew out a quizzical breath, as if
waiting for her reply.

"I-I'm Steph. Steph Danes. I'm . . . um,
here for a riding lesson," she found herself
stammering.

"I am honored to meet you, Steph,"
Comet said, bowing his head.

"M-Me too," Steph said, still not quite
believing this was happening. Talking ponies
belonged in fairy tales or fantasy movies.
"Where did you say you came from?"

"Rainbow Mist Island. It is a place far
away, where I live with the other Lightning
Horses."

Steph's curiosity was starting to get the better of her shock. "So . . . how come you're here in Marshall's Stables?"

Comet glanced around at his surroundings. His long lashes blinked as he looked over the brick walls and clean straw on the floor. "Is that where I am? I have come to find Destiny, my twin sister."

"Is she here at the riding stable, too?" Steph asked.

"No, I do not think she is here in these stables, but she is hiding somewhere nearby in your world," Comet explained with a flick of his black tail. "She fled after she accidentally lost the Stone of Power, which protects our Lightning Herd. My twin sister and I were cloud-racing in the night sky when she dropped the stone. She thought it was lost forever. I found it, but Destiny does not know this. She is afraid to come home because she thinks she is in a lot of trouble."

Steph nodded slowly. "You say you and Destiny were *cloud-racing*? But how . . . ?"

"I will show you," Comet said, backing away.

Steph felt a strange warm tingling

sensation flow down to her fingertips
as violet-colored sparkles glittered in
Comet's black-and-white coat and streaks
of rainbow mist wove around him. The
handsome piebald pony disappeared and
in its place, almost filling the loose box,
stood an elegant young cream-colored
pony with a flowing gold mane and tail.

Springing from its shoulders were folded wings, covered with shimmering golden feathers.

"Oh!" Steph caught her breath. She had never seen anything so wonderful in her entire life.

"Comet?" she gasped.

"Yes, Steph. It is still me. Do not be afraid." Comet gave a deep, musical whinny.

Before Steph could get used to the sight of the beautiful winged pony, there was a final swirl of sparkling mist and Comet reappeared as the handsome black-and-white piebald pony.

"That's a great disguise! Can Destiny make herself look like an ordinary pony, too?" Steph asked.

Comet nodded slowly. "Yes, but that

will not save her if the dark horses who want to steal our magic discover her," he explained. "I must find Destiny and take her back to Rainbow Mist Island before they do. Will you help me?"

Steph thought about it. Her heart was still aching for Fleur, so she knew how it felt to miss someone she loved. "Okay, I'll search for Destiny with you," she decided. To her surprise, she was actually starting to feel quite proud that this amazing magic pony had chosen to reveal himself to her. "Wait until I tell Mom and Dad about you. They won't believe it—"

"No. You cannot tell anyone about me or what I have told you!" Comet looked at her with serious eyes.

Steph felt disappointed. She was already keeping a secret about how much she

missed Fleur from her mom and dad;
she felt bad keeping another. But Comet
was right, this probably wasn't the sort of
thing that a grown-up would believe!

"You must promise me," Comet
insisted gently.

"Well . . . okay then. Cross my heart.
No one's going to hear about you from
me." Steph was prepared to agree if it
would help protect Comet and Destiny
until they returned together to Rainbow
Mist Island.

"Steph? Are you still here?" Judy
Marshall's voice rang out as she strode
across the stable yard, obviously having
finished her telephone conversation.

Inside the loose box, Steph tensed.
Judy was going to see her with Comet at
any moment!

In an attempt to hide the magic pony, she shot outside, closed the door and stood with her back pressed against it. Comet seemed to think it was some kind of game and leaned over her shoulder to nuzzle her hair.

"There you are!" Judy said, smiling. "What's so interesting about that empty box? I thought you'd have chosen a pony and tacked it up by now."

Empty box? Steph could feel Comet's warm breath tickling her neck. But, for some reason, Judy didn't seem to be able to see him.

"I have used my magic, so that only you can see and hear me," Comet whinnied softly in her ear.

"Oh!" Steph just about managed not to jump out of her skin. "Oh, right. Cool!"

She gave Judy a huge cheesy grin. "I
mean . . . um . . . The ponies are all cool.
I can't decide which one to ride." She
pointed hastily toward a large gray pony
in the nearest box. "I . . . um . . . think
I'd like to ride that one, please."

"Good choice," Judy said, grinning at
her enthusiasm. "Misty's just the right size
for you. You'll find her very responsive.
I'll show you where her tack is."

Steph followed Judy into the tack
room and emerged a few moments later
carrying a saddle, with a bridle looped
over her arm. Judy had led the gray pony
out and secured her to a metal ring in
the wall.

As Steph began tacking up Misty,
Judy stood by. She nodded with approval.
"You seem to know what you're doing."

"I started riding when I was five years old," Steph said. She caught a movement from the corner of her eye and only just managed to suppress a gasp. Comet's head was pushing through the loose-box door. His neck, front legs and the rest of him followed and then he stood waiting calmly, while Steph buckled on her riding hat and mounted Misty.

She wasn't sure whether to laugh or pinch herself to see if she was dreaming.

Judy hadn't noticed anything unusual. "You can take Misty along the bridle path that leads down to the canal. Do you know it?"

Steph nodded. "I used to ride Fleur, my old pony, along that path beside the canal. It's a great ride." She felt a wave of sadness as she thought again about riding Fleur.

"Yes, it is," Judy agreed. "You'll know the pedestrian bridge then. Cross over the canal there and then come back to the stables. Okay?"

"All right. Thanks, Judy. See you later." Steph patted the gray mare's neck as she used her heels to nudge her forward.

As she, Misty, and Comet trotted out of the stable yard and headed for the bridle path, Steph smiled to herself.

She was glad that her dad had persuaded her to try out the new riding stables in an attempt to cheer her up. She hadn't forgotten about Fleur, like he seemed to hope she would, but Steph had a sneaking suspicion that this amazing magic pony might turn out to be a very special friend!

Chapter
THREE

Misty was a smooth ride and Steph relaxed in the saddle as she continued along the bridle path with Comet at her side. The sky was bright blue and bees buzzed among the colorful wild flowers that dotted the grass on either side.

Comet looked around, scanning the countryside with keen bright eyes for any sign of Destiny. Steph peered into

the bushes and hedges as they passed,
keeping her eyes open, too.

The bridle path followed the curve
of a valley on its way down to the canal.
There were fields of bright yellow flowers
on one side. A bit further on, they passed
acres of dusty-green ripening corn and
then came to some clumps of trees.

Comet saw a movement in a thicket
of birches and galloped off to investigate.

Steph halted Misty. She was deciding whether to leave the path and follow him when Comet appeared through the trees and came back toward her.

"It was only someone walking their dog," he told her sadly.

Steph could see that his deep-violet eyes were shadowed by disappointment. "I'm sorry you didn't find Destiny," she said gently. "But there are lots of other places to look."

Comet nodded, and his black mane swung forward. "At least I can be sure that Destiny did not pass by this way."

"How can you know that?" Steph asked curiously.

"Destiny and I have a special bond because we are twins. If she is close, I will sense her presence. Also, if she has passed by at any time, she will have left a trail."

"Do you mean like broken stalks and stuff?" Steph guessed.

"No. There will be dimly glowing hoofprints, which are invisible to most people in your world."

"Will I be able to see them?"

"Only if you are riding with me or we are very close," Comet told her. "I think because you are special enough to see me that you will be able to see Destiny's hoofprints, too."

Steph smiled. She was growing very fond of Comet.

The magic pony pawed at the grass with one front hoof. "Are you ready to go on, Steph? I would like to keep searching."

"Sure. Let's go!" Steph squeezed Misty, letting her know she was ready to move on.

They reached the part of the track that led to the canal. Steph turned Misty on to the old path. Comet followed, his mane and tail stirring in the warm breeze.

Brightly painted houseboats with cheerful rose and castle designs were moored alongside the canal. Some of them had window boxes and pots filled with red and orange flowers. Longer black barges slid through the greenish water. People called out and waved as Steph rode along.

Steph waved back, feeling a surge of happiness. It was a perfect day for doing what she loved best in the whole world. Riding! Especially with the magic pony who had chosen her to be his special friend.

They passed fields and then some buildings and a yard filled with lorries. Some time later, they rounded a bend. "There's the bridge," Steph said, pointing ahead. "We have to go across it."

Comet pricked his ears eagerly. "It looks high up."

Steph nodded. "It is. You can see a long way from up there."

The bridge was very old, with painted cast-iron railings. Misty's hooves clip-clopped on the wooden boards, but Comet's made no sound.

"I can't see any ponies in the fields, can you?" Steph asked Comet as they paused in the middle to look out over the canal.

"No, I cannot." Comet turned his head to look toward the marina on one side, where the masts of many sailing boats seemed to prick the sky. In the other direction were houses and a dark-green forest behind them. His eyes lit up with interest as he looked at the thick trees. "That would be a good place for Destiny to hide," he neighed.

"I'm supposed to go back to the stables now," Steph said. "But I could try to sneak out and meet you later, and then we can go and look together."

Comet nodded. "You could ride on my back. We would travel more quickly that way."

"Oh wow. Really?" Steph felt a thrill
at the thought of riding the magic pony.
She was surprised to realize that she
couldn't wait.

They picked up the bridle path again
after crossing the bridge. As the riding

stables came into view, Steph had a sudden
thought.

"Where are you going to stay?" she
asked Comet. "You can't live at the riding
stables. They'll probably put another pony
in that empty box."

Comet flicked one ear as he turned to
look at her. "You are right, Steph. I will
come home with you," he decided.

"Really? Oh, I'd love that," Steph
cried. "You can stay in Fleur's old stable."
Steph was sure that Fleur wouldn't have
minded. "It's perfect! And I can spend
tons of time with you and we can go out
looking for Destiny together—" She broke
off as she realized there was a snag in her
plan. "Except that I don't see how I can
get you to our house. You don't know the
way. And you can't gallop behind the car,

it's too dangerous. I know! I'll call Dad
and tell him I'm walking home. It's not
that far. Then I can ride you."

Comet nodded, looking pleased.

"It's settled then," Steph said happily.

But as she reached the stable's parking
lot, she groaned. "Oh no! Too late. There's
our car."

Mr. Danes saw her riding. He got
out of the car and stood waiting as she
rode Misty into the yard. "Hi, Steph!" he
called, waving.

Steph forced a smile as she waved back.
"Now what are we going to do?" she
murmured, looking sideways at Comet.

The magic pony flicked his tail and
gave her a mysterious smile. She felt faint
tingles flowing down her fingers. Before
she could ask what was going on, her

magic pony had disappeared, leaving only the tiniest shower of violet sparks.

Chapter
FOUR

"So did you have a good time?" Steph's dad wanted to know as they drove home.

"Yes, thanks. It was . . . um . . . great. Judy was really friendly and Misty's a great pony," Steph said, mustering up all the enthusiasm she could. It had been really kind of her dad to arrange the surprise for her, and she didn't want to seem ungrateful. His plan had worked in a way;

she was starting to feel better about not having Fleur around. But now she was worried about Comet. Where had he gone so suddenly?

Maybe she would never see him again.

He's probably changed his mind about coming home with me and decided to look for his twin sister all by himself from now on, she thought glumly.

Steph shifted uncomfortably in her seat. A lump in her jeans pocket was pressing into her leg. What could it be? She didn't remember putting a tissue or anything in there. Puzzled, she slipped her hand into the pocket and felt her fingers close around something very small and soft.

Steph drew the tiny object out and her eyes widened in surprise as she saw what she was holding. It was a miniature soft toy pony. As she gazed at it, the fluffy little black-and-white pony shook itself and blinked at her with bead-bright violet eyes.

"Comet!" She gasped, and then quickly turned it into sneeze. "Ah-choo!"

"Bless you," her dad said.

Comet stretched his neck to look up at her. "I found another way of coming home with you!" he told Steph in a miniature neigh that matched his new size.

She smiled down at him delightedly. Comet was unbelievably beautiful as his real winged self, and handsome as a black-and-white pony—but right now he was the sweetest, most gorgeous fluffy miniature pony she had ever seen.

Her dad looked back at her for a second. "Cute toy. Did Judy give you that?" he asked.

Steph thought fast. "Um . . . yeah! They're giving them to all the new customers. It's to . . . um . . . to help advertise the new stables," she improvised.

Her dad nodded slowly. "That's a great idea. Very enterprising."

Steph realized that Comet's magic must be working again; making sure that only she could see that the tiny toy was alive.

The moment she got home, Steph said a quick hello to her mom and then made an excuse about having to clean some of Fleur's tack. She rushed straight outside to the stable. Once there, she gently put Comet on the floor, where he seemed even tinier in the empty stall.

Steph felt a stronger warm tingling flow to the very tips of her fingers. The toy horse's black-and-white fur glittered with miniature sparkles like violet fairy

lights. A faint rainbow mist spread
outward and suddenly Comet appeared as
a normal-size black-and-white pony.

Steph went forward and threw her
arms around his neck. "That was amazing!
You're full of surprises!" she said, laying

her cheek against his warm, satiny skin.
"I'm so glad you decided to come home
with me. I think it's best if you stay
invisible, so Mom or Dad don't see you
and ask awkward questions."

Comet gave a soft, contented blow. "I
think so, too."

As Steph lowered her arms and stood
back, Comet raised his head and swiveled
his ears. He peered intently toward the
open door.

"What is it?" she asked him, turning
to look down the side of the house. From
here she had a restricted view of the cul-
de-sac.

"I hear hoofbeats approaching," he
told her in an urgent little neigh.

"But I'm the only person in Porlock
Close who owned a pony." Steph caught

her breath as a thought struck her. "What if it's Destiny? Maybe *she's* found *you*!"

"I do hope so! I have missed her so much." Comet's eyes glowed like amethysts. He trotted outside eagerly.

Steph followed more slowly. If it *was* Destiny, maybe Comet would take her straight back with him to Rainbow Mist Island. She felt a pang as she realized that she'd barely gotten used to having Comet for a friend. She certainly wasn't ready to lose him so soon.

As Steph and Comet reached the front drive, a girl on a stunning dark bay pony rode up to them.

Comet's head drooped slightly and his eyes lost a little of their color. "That is not Destiny," he whinnied sadly.

"I'm sorry you're disappointed," Steph

said soothingly, feeling guilty at her sense
of relief that he would be staying with
her. "Don't forget we're going to check
out those woods we saw from the canal
bridge."

Comet nodded, his eyes glistening
with renewed hope.

The girl drew her pony to a halt.
"Hi! Found you at last!" she said with
a friendly smile. She looked at Steph,
unable to see Comet, who stood next
to her. "I've noticed you riding past our
house a few times on your chestnut pony
and wanted to meet you. I don't know
anyone else around here who owns a
pony. I'm Ellie Browning."

"Hi, Ellie," Steph said. "I'm Stephanie
Danes, but everyone calls me Steph." She
looked admiringly at the elegant bay.

"Your pony's gorgeous. What's his name?"

"Turpin," Ellie said proudly, tossing back the long dark-red hair that streamed out from under her riding hat. "He's an Arab. I haven't had him that long."

"Hello, Turpin." Steph held out her hand, so the pony could get her scent. He was the color of strong coffee and his mane and tail were almost black.

"Would you like to come over to my house?" Ellie invited. "We can put the ponies through their paces. It'll be fun. We've just moved into the old house near the village green."

Steph knew that Ellie was referring to Fleur, as she couldn't see Comet. She tried not to feel too sad and she hoped the little chestnut was settling in with her new owner.

She knew Ellie's house. It was very large, with a stone porch and pillars beside the red front door. A row of small trees, clipped into triangles, lined the smart drive. There were usually expensive cars parked there.

"I'd love to come, but I don't have a pony now." *At least, not one I can tell you about*, she thought. "I just had to sell

Fleur. I got too big for her," she told Ellie.

"Oh, that's a shame. You must miss her," Ellie said sympathetically. "Turpin's my first pony. At my old house, I always rode riding-school ponies. But we've got a lot of space now, so Mom and Dad bought me my very own pony. Why don't you come over anyway? We can take turns riding Turpin."

Steph smiled, liking Ellie more and more. She hoped they would become friends. She felt excited by the idea of riding the little Arab pony. "I'd love to. When should I come over?"

Ellie put her head on one side. "Let's see. Tomorrow's Sunday, so I have to visit my grandma, who lives hours away. How about Monday? It's a holiday, so we can have the whole day together."

"Great!" Steph said.

They decided on a time and then Steph stood by as Ellie clicked her tongue at Turpin and squeezed him on. Steph watched until they rode out of Porlock Close.

"She seems really nice, doesn't she?" Steph said to Comet.

"I liked her, too."

Steph thought he sounded a little sad after the false alarm and was probably

thinking about his missing twin. She reached up to pat his shoulder as they walked back to the stable, promising herself that she'd get up extra early the following morning so they could go out searching for Destiny.

Chapter
FIVE

Sunday morning dawned bright and clear.

It was only just light when Steph woke and put on her jeans and T-shirt quickly. Dashing downstairs, she grabbed her riding boots and hat from the utility room and then hurried outside to the stable.

Comet whinnied a soft welcome as soon as he saw her.

"Are you ready to go? I think we have a couple of hours before Mom and Dad get up. We can check out those woods we saw from the canal bridge."

The magic pony pushed his velvety nose into her hand, his deep-violet eyes sparkling with affection. "Thank you, Steph. Climb onto my back."

Steph mounted. She twined her hands in Comet's thick mane as he leaped forward and galloped down the side of the house.

The streets were calm and almost empty. Comet sped along, his hooves making no sound on the pavement. He was exciting to ride and as fast as the wind.

Steph bit back a gasp of excitement as she crouched low on his back. Houses, shops, the canal, and hedges all whooshed past in a sparkly blur and then they were out in the open countryside.

Faster, ever faster, Comet raced. His magic seemed to spread over Steph like a warm cloak and she felt safe and secure astride him—almost as if she was surrounded by a protective bubble of rainbow magic. Comet slowed his pace as they entered the woods and began to weave along the paths through the trees.

Steph looked from left to right, searching for evidence that a pony might have taken cover there, but there was no sign of Destiny or any trace of glowing hoofprints.

Comet stretched his neck and raked the bushes and tangles of undergrowth with his keen eyes.

After carefully searching every inch of the woods, they had to admit defeat.

"The morning mist has dried and the sun is high in the sky," Comet pointed out to Steph as they stood at the top of a steep bank. "I will take you back now."

Steph could have gone on riding Comet for hours. "Okay." She patted his neck reassuringly. Steph knew that her mom and dad would be getting up soon anyway. "We can go out searching again tomorrow, when we go over to Ellie's house."

Comet wheeled around and was about to retrace his steps when a gust of wind came out of nowhere. Suddenly, a white plastic bag flew out of a bush and wrapped around his front legs. With a squeal of alarm, Comet reared up, kicking out and trying to dislodge the scary thing he thought was attacking him.

"Oh!" Taken by surprise, Steph lost her grip on his mane. She slid down his back and luckily managed to land on her feet.

"It's okay, Comet. It's only a bag. It won't hurt you!" she cried.

In his panic Comet didn't seem to hear

her. He snorted and edged backward until
he was in danger of slipping down the
side of the bank.

He would hurt himself if he fell!
Steph thought fast. Grabbing a tree
branch from the ground, she dashed
beneath his flailing hooves and hooked
the plastic bag with the twig.

"Yes!" she cried, as she pulled it free,
bundled it up, and stuffed it into her jeans
pocket.

But as Steph took a step back, she stumbled and felt herself falling.

"Oh!" She tumbled over and over down the slope. One of her arms hit a large stone and pain shot through her.

Biting her lip, Steph struggled to her feet, quickly climbed back up, and then staggered over to sit on a fallen log. To her relief, Comet seemed unharmed.

The magic pony's sides heaved as he gradually calmed down. He looked around for Steph and walked over to where she was sitting. Leaning down, he gently snuffled her shoulder, surrounding her with sweet hay-scented breath.

"Thank you, Steph. It was very brave of you to help me."

"I couldn't bear it if anything happened to you. I thought you were going to

tumble down that bank," she said. "Oh!"
she gasped, holding her numb arm. Now
that the excitement was over, it was
beginning to throb painfully.

"You are hurt!" Comet said. "I will
help you."

He blew out another warm breath. This
time it twinkled with a million tiny violet
stars. The sparkly healing mist swirled
around Steph's arm for a few moments
before it sank into it and disappeared. She
felt the pain in her numb arm increase a
little before suddenly draining away like
water gurgling down a drain.

"Oh, thank you, Comet. I feel much
better!" she said, stroking the broad white
stripe on his nose.

"Good." He snorted affectionately. "I
am glad to be able to take care of you. And

I will always do so while I am here."

Steph looked up at him adoringly. "I hope you'll live here with me forever. And there's room for Destiny, too. You could both stay."

"That is not possible," Comet neighed softly. "We must return to our family on Rainbow Mist Island. Do you understand that, Steph?"

Steph nodded slowly, feeling her chest tighten with sadness.

She realized how fond of him she'd become. Comet had gradually filled the space left in her heart by Fleur. The thought of one day losing him was too painful to think about. She decided not to dwell on that now and, instead, to enjoy every single moment she could.

Comet whickered and reached out to

nudge her arm gently. "Climb onto me again, Steph,"

She mounted and he sprang forward. The journey home was even faster. Time seemed almost to stand still and then Steph was beside the magic pony again in the stable. "I'll come out and see you later," she promised, before hurrying into the house.

She was pouring cereal into a bowl
for breakfast in the kitchen when she
heard her mom coming down the stairs.

"Hello, sweetie!" Mrs. Danes said,
blinking in surprise as she walked over to
turn the coffeemaker on. "Why are you
up so early?"

*You'd never believe me, even if I could tell
you!* Steph thought, biting back a secret
grin. "Oh, no reason really. I just couldn't
sleep in on such a beautiful day!" she said
casually.

Chapter
SIX

Steph set out early on Comet to
ride over and see Ellie at her house the
following day. Comet's magic made sure
that they were invisible to everyone for
the whole ride.

As Steph had promised him, they
took the opportunity to check out the
village streets for signs of Destiny, but
there was still no trace of Comet's twin

sister. Steph dismounted at the back of the quiet churchyard and then Comet walked invisibly beside her as she called for Ellie.

Mrs. Browning opened the door. "Hello, you must be Steph. Nice to meet you."

"Hello, Mrs. Browning," Steph said politely.

"Ellie told me that you just had to sell
your pony. That's a shame."

"I know. I really miss her," Steph
told Ellie's mom, feeling a lump rise in
her throat. "I had Fleur for three years,
but she went to a really good home." She
took a deep breath and quickly changed
the subject. "Ellie seems thrilled with
Turpin. He's a gorgeous pony."

"Yes, he is. Ellie loves him to pieces.
I'm not sure that she quite understands
what looking after him involves yet,
though. I suspect most girls are like that
with their first ponies."

"I guess some are," Steph agreed. "I
always loved everything about looking
after ponies and horses. I want to work
with them when I grow up."

"Good for you. Perhaps you can give

Ellie a few tips. She's with Turpin now. I'll
open the side gate so you can walk down
the garden to the stable." Mrs. Browning
came outside and Steph followed her.

The back garden was enormous, with
tennis courts, a summer house, and a
swimming pool. The stable was on the
other side. It was an impressive redbrick
building beside a large paddock.

"Wow! Just look at this place," Steph
whispered to Comet, her eyes widening.

Comet glanced around. "It is very
nice here. But I like my stable at the place
where you live."

"I'm glad, because I love having you
living with me!" Steph threw him an
adoring look.

"Hi, Steph!" Ellie appeared at the
stable door. She wore a blue T-shirt with

a designer pony logo, jodhpurs, and boots. "Come on in."

Inside the stable, Steph caught her breath. There was room here for two ponies. Another door led to a tack room and feed store, with a counter and a deep sink. Yet another door led to a toilet with a washbasin.

Steph shaped her lips into a silent whistle. "This is like a palace!" It would be a dream to keep a pony in a place like this.

Ellie smiled. "I know. I'm really lucky to have it. Mom says that Dad got a bit carried away when he had it built."

Steph laughed.

She hoped again that they might become good friends. It would be fun for her and Comet to spend time with Ellie and Turpin.

Turpin was in one of the stalls. His
ears twitched inquisitively and he turned
his supple neck to look at them.

"Hello, beautiful," Steph said. He
really was a good-looking pony. She
loved Arabs; they had such elegant heads
and big soft eyes.

As she went closer to pat him, she
frowned. There were traces of dried mud

on his legs and bits of twig and grass in his tail. His bay coat was a bit dull, too.

Steph's fingers itched for her grooming kit. She would love to be let loose on Turpin. She imagined untangling his mane and tail and spraying conditioner on them, before brushing his entire coffee-colored coat until it was smooth and glossy.

"Oh, Turpin," Ellie scolded gently. "You haven't touched your new hay net. You're not feeling all moody, are you?"

Steph glanced into the stall and immediately saw that the hay net had been hung up too high and Turpin was straining to reach it.

"You need to bring the net down a bit, so he can get to it more easily," she said without thinking. "Ponies can get grass seeds in their eyes with the net above them."

Ellie reddened. "I knew that," she snapped, going into the stall to adjust it.

Steph bit her lip. She remembered what Mrs. Browning had said about Ellie not being all that used to the hard work of looking after a pony. Maybe it would be best to go easy with the advice.

But she couldn't help noticing a heap of bridles lying in a tangle on the floor. Two expensive horse blankets had been dumped in a corner, despite the blanket box standing open.

Comet blew air from his nostrils and wrinkled his lips at the slight tang of soiled straw.

"Yes, I can smell it, too," Steph whispered to him. "I don't think Ellie

realizes that you have to do regular poo
picking." She turned to Ellie. "Where do
you keep your fork and skip? I'll give you
a hand to pick up those fresh droppings.
I know it's a bit boring having to do it all
the time. But it's one of those things you
can't get out of." She rolled her eyes, as if
she found it a chore, too.

"Tell me about it!" Ellie said with
feeling as she led Turpin out of his stall.

"I didn't realize how much hard
work it was to look after your own pony.
Mom and Dad say that Turpin's my
responsibility, so I have to learn to do it by
myself." She sighed. "Anyway, leave those
droppings for now. I'll clean them up later
before I get Turpin in for the night. Let's
go and have some fun with him. Aren't
you dying to ride him?"

"You bet!" Steph said, deciding not
to nag about cleaning up, in case Ellie
got annoyed again. Anyway, she was
really excited to try out her new friend's
Arab pony.

Ellie put Turpin into the paddock
and Steph and Comet followed them in.

The magic pony immediately cantered
across the grass and then lay down.
Snorting happily, Comet rolled onto his

back, all four legs waving in the air.

Steph hid a smile, pleased that Comet was enjoying himself.

With an eager nicker, Turpin trotted over and sniffed Comet curiously. Comet got to his feet and shook himself, his dark mane flying outward. He reached out and snuffled Turpin's neck.

Steph watched delightedly as the ponies got acquainted. Maybe Comet wouldn't miss Destiny so much if he made a new pony friend.

Kicking up their heels, Turpin and Comet cantered down to the other side of the paddock and then stood side by side, cropping the grass.

Ellie frowned. "He's never gone rushing off like that before. Come here, Turpin! Come on, boy!" she encouraged.

Turpin twitched his ears. He looked toward Ellie and then lowered his head again.

Ellie sighed and began stomping toward him. Turpin eyed her. He waited until she got within a couple of feet and then danced away with his tail jinked up in the air.

Ellie stopped, waiting until her pony began to crop the grass again before advancing. The same thing happened. Turpin stayed where he was until Ellie was almost within reach, then flicked his tail up and shot away again.

Steph laughed, guessing that this could go on for some time.

"Hey! It's not funny!" Ellie cried, annoyed. "Dumb pony! What's wrong with him today?"

"He's just being silly!" Steph said. *And showing off in front of Comet!* "I could show you a trick to get him to come to you, if you like."

Ellie looked intrigued. "Go on."

Steph moved forward a few paces. She

waved her arms in the air to get Turpin's attention. When he looked at her, she turned her back. Crouching down, she pretended to be looking at something in the grass.

"Wow! Look at this," she said enthusiastically.

"What's there? I can't see anything," Ellie said.

"That's because there's nothing there! But Turpin doesn't know that. He won't be able to resist coming over to see what I'm doing," Steph explained, chancing a furtive look over her shoulder.

She saw Turpin's ears twitch forward. He snorted softly and took a few steps forward.

"It's working!" Ellie whispered as the little Arab pony kept coming.

Steph waited until Turpin stopped and stretched his neck toward her. Very slowly, she reached up and took hold of his head collar, at the same time rising smoothly to her feet.

"Clever boy," she praised, rubbing his satiny cheek.

Ellie looked impressed. "That's a neat trick. I'd never have thought of that. How come you know so much about ponies?"

Steph was glad that Ellie seemed to have calmed down a bit with her. "I love learning new stuff. I'm weird like that!" she joked modestly. "Is it okay if we ride Turpin now?"

"Sure. Go for it. You first," Ellie said generously.

Steph swung herself up. The Arab pony was just the right size for her. She settled herself comfortably, urging Turpin into a trot and then a canter. He had a smooth, even stride and was alert and responsive to her commands.

"Turpin's a dream to ride. He's exactly the sort of pony I'd like next," she said to Ellie as she dismounted. "He's so sweet-natured and intelligent. Are you going to show him?"

"I might. I haven't decided yet," Ellie said evasively.

Steph widened her eyes. "Oh, you totally have to! He's a real winner!" she enthused.

"I think so, too!" Ellie said, smiling, but then she wrinkled her nose. "But it's a bit of a sore point right now. My parents won't let me enter any competitions until I'm better at taking care of Turpin. Can you believe that?"

Steph knew not to say anything. From the little she'd already seen, she thought Ellie had some way to go before her parents felt that she was a competent pony owner. But she didn't want to say so, in case Ellie got defensive with her again.

Ellie had mounted Turpin and was riding him around the paddock. Steph watched, impressed. There was nothing

wrong with Ellie's riding skills. She
was confident, perfectly in control, and
sensitive to her mount.

Ellie's face was glowing as she cantered
back to where Steph was waiting.

"Isn't he incredible?" she said, leaning
over to pat her pony's neck.

"He certainly is," Steph agreed
admiringly.

Then it was her turn to ride Turpin again.

At the end of the afternoon, Steph was feeling relaxed and full of the afterglow of a few hours of enjoyable riding. As Ellie went to lead her pony back to his stable, she made a suggestion.

"Why don't we leave both ponies in the paddock and I'll help you do Turpin's bedding and clear things up?"

A puzzled look crossed Ellie's face. "Ponies? There's only one in the paddock! Unless one of them is invisible!"

"Oh yeah! Silly me!" Steph said quickly, glancing at Comet, who was cheekily flicking one ear toward her. "It must be wishful thinking. I guess I'm still missing Fleur! So, about Turpin's bedding . . ."

Ellie sighed deeply. "Don't you start bossing me around, too! It's bad enough having Mom and Dad always at me!" she grumbled.

"I wasn't . . . I wouldn't . . . !" Steph countered, feeling herself starting to get annoyed at last. She'd done all she could to be friendly, but Ellie seemed determined to take everything the wrong way. "I guess I should go then. See you later," she called out shortly as she walked away.

There was no answer from Ellie.

Chapter SEVEN

"How did you get along with Ellie?" Steph's dad asked that evening as they sat around the table having dinner.

"We had a . . . um . . . good time," Steph said. She was already regretting leaving so abruptly. "I enjoyed riding Turpin. He's a really nice pony. I think we're going to meet up again tomorrow afternoon near the woods behind her house." *At least I hope we are*, she thought, *unless Ellie is still mad at me.*

"Lucky you. I'm glad you've found a new friend with a pony. Especially one who lives nearby," her mom commented.

They finished eating, and Steph helped clear away the dishes. There were some bits of apple and carrot left over from the salad. Without thinking, she slipped them into her pocket for Comet.

Her dad raised his eyebrows at her in surprise.

"I . . . um . . . might need a snack later," Steph said hurriedly. "At least it's better than eating sweets."

"Maybe I should follow your lead," her dad said, patting his round tummy.

Mrs. Danes laughed. "Well, it wouldn't hurt you. Just kidding!" she said as her husband grimaced. She looked at Steph. "I know you're still missing Fleur, but I wondered whether we should start looking for a bigger and more challenging pony for you. What do you think?"

Steph considered this carefully. Was she ready to look for another pony to take the little chestnut's place? Did she even want a brand-new pony to look after and love, now that she had Comet in her life?

But Steph knew that Comet was also
a Lightning Horse who lived in another
world and could never belong to her—
not like a pony of her own.

She made a decision. "Okay, but if
I have a new pony, I'd like one just like
Turpin. Everything about him is great."

"I got a brief glimpse of Ellie on the
front drive. That little Arab's a stunner,
all right," her dad agreed. "I can see why
you're so taken with him. But I'm not
sure we can afford a pony of his breeding
right now."

"That's okay. I don't mind waiting,"
Steph said helpfully. *Perfect!* she thought.
It would probably give her time to get
used to the idea of riding a new pony.

Her mom looked surprised. "Are you
sure? It might take us a while to save up."

"No problem! I can always go to the riding school. They have some really nice ponies," Steph replied.

"And maybe Ellie will let you ride Turpin now and then," her dad added.

Steph said nothing. She wasn't so sure about that. She and Ellie weren't exactly getting along.

But her parents seemed happy with their decision. So it was settled.

Once her mom had left for her monthly book group and her dad was tinkering about in the garden shed, Steph slipped outside to give Comet his treats.

He crunched up the apple and carrots with his strong teeth. "Delicious! Thank you, Steph."

"You're welcome." She threaded her fingers through his thick black mane,

stroking it flat as she told him about the
conversation with her mom and dad.
"I hope we get to meet up with Ellie
and Turpin again, don't you?" she said
wistfully.

Comet nodded, chewing.

"Ellie might not want to be friends with me now. She thinks I boss her around, like her parents. But I only wanted to help. There's a lot to learn about when you get your first pony." She sighed. "I wish I knew how to make her like me again."

"You will find a way, Steph," Comet neighed confidently.

Steph leaned forward and Comet cantered along. Her fingers tingled slightly as his warm magic swirled around her again. They were on their way to meet Ellie and Turpin near the woods— hopefully.

Despite worrying about whether Ellie would show up, Steph felt a burst of pure happiness. Riding Comet was so

wonderful. She knew she'd never get
bored of it.

They soon reached the wooded area.
Wide paths wound among the birches and
field maples, and there was a flat grassed
area with a shallow pond in the center.

Steph looked around, but she couldn't
see Ellie and Turpin. She didn't mind if
they were late. It meant she would have
longer to ride Comet before she had to
find somewhere out of sight to dismount
and become visible again.

Comet moved along a grass path, bars
of sunlight and shade striping his smooth
patched coat.

"It's really pretty here, isn't it? Oh!"
Steph gasped.

She only just managed to keep from
slipping sideways as Comet came to

a sudden halt. He stretched his neck forward to snuffle at the ground.

"Comet? What's going on?" She glanced down to see a faint line of softly glowing violet hoofprints. They led between the trees and stretched away into the distance.

"Destiny! She has been here!" Comet neighed joyfully.

Did that mean that Comet was leaving to go after her? "Is she close? Can you tell where she is?" Steph asked him anxiously.

Comet shook his head. "The trail is cold. But I know now that Destiny came this way. When I am very close to catching up with her, I will be able to hear her hoofbeats. And then I may have to leave suddenly, without saying good-bye."

"Oh." Steph felt a tug of dismay as she realized that she would never be ready to lose her magical friend. "Are you sure that you and Destiny wouldn't like to stay here and live with me?" she asked in a small voice.

Comet shook his head, his eyes softening. "We must return to our family on Rainbow Mist Island," he reminded her gently.

Steph nodded sadly. "Destiny must be missing her home after being lost for so long." Her eyes stung with tears, but she knew that she must face the truth, however hard it was. Besides, Comet wasn't leaving yet. There was still time to enjoy every moment spent with him.

She saw something from the corner of her eye as a pony and rider approached the woods. It was Ellie and Turpin.

Comet quickly slipped behind a thick bush, and Steph slid from his back. There was a tiny spurt of violet sparkles as she became visible again.

Steph stepped out and began walking toward Ellie. "Hi! Ellie! I'm over here!" she called delightedly.

"Steph!" Ellie called, a note of

urgency in her voice. She encouraged
Turpin into a trot. "I . . . I'm sorry I was
a pain yesterday. Can we still be friends?"

"You bet!" Steph said happily.

She frowned as they rode up. Turpin
looked a bit strange. She couldn't see
why, until Ellie reined him in.

Turpin had just been clipped. Cutting
the pony's coat using electric clippers

was something only experienced owners attempted.

Steph had never seen such a botched job. A good clip left smooth skin and neat areas of unclipped longer coat. Poor Turpin had random wobbly lines cut through his coat on his sides and back.

"Oh my goodness! Who did that?" Steph asked, horrified.

Ellie's face said it all.

"*You* did it? But why?" Steph blinked her friend in amazement. She couldn't believe that Ellie had attempted something so complicated.

Ellie rolled her eyes. "Mom and Dad were bugging me *again* about how I had to learn how to look after Turpin properly. So I thought I'd impress them by giving him a clip. I read how to do it in one of my pony magazines, and it looked really easy. But I couldn't get it to look right. Then the clippers went blunt and I couldn't find the spare blades."

"Well, you can't leave him like that," Steph said, aghast. "It looks like moths have been chomping him!"

Ellie's face fell. "If you're just going to make fun—"

"I'm not," Steph cut in quickly, wishing that she'd bitten her tongue. Ellie was obviously upset, although trying hard not to show it, and she didn't want them to fall out again. Especially since they'd only just made up after last time. "Um . . . is there anything I can do to help?"

"Yes. You can clip him properly for me," Ellie stated.

"What!" Steph looked at her in horror.

Clipping a pony was really complicated and could take ages. "I helped while Fleur was clipped once, so I know what to do. But I don't think I'm up to doing the whole thing by myself."

"You have to try! Please!" Ellie begged. "Mom and Dad are out, but they'll be back soon. They'll go nuts if they see Turpin looking like this."

Steph felt squeezed into a corner. She guessed that Ellie wasn't exaggerating; she was already on thin ice with her parents where Turpin was concerned.

"Well—okay then," Steph decided reluctantly. "I'll just have to do my best. I'll get my grooming kit and meet you at your house."

Ellie beamed at her in relief. "Thanks, Steph. You'll be as quick as you can, right?"

"Okay." Steph let out a sigh of exasperation as Ellie rode away. "I must be crazy. It's going to take a miracle to make Turpin look even half decent. That's if I even have time to get started before Ellie's mom and dad see him!"

"I will help you," Comet neighed.

"Thanks, Comet. What would I do without you?" Steph smiled gratefully at her magical friend.

Chapter
EIGHT

As soon as Ellie couldn't see her, Steph mounted Comet and held on tightly. Rainbow streaks glittered in the magic pony's flowing black mane and tail as he galloped at the speed of light toward Steph's house. They picked up the plastic box with her grooming kit and clippers and quickly set off back to Ellie's before Steph's mom and dad realized she'd been there.

On arriving at Ellie's, Comet's
shining hooves barely brushed the
ground as he galloped into the paddock
behind the stable and stopped for Steph
to dismount.

Steph immediately became visible
and ran toward the stable door. Comet
followed by her side. They had only

taken a few steps when they heard raised voices.

Steph caught her breath in alarm. "Uh-oh! It sounds like Ellie's mom and dad have come back early," she whispered.

Mr. Browning's angry voice floated out of the open door. "Honestly, Ellie. Look at this place. There's stuff lying about everywhere. Turpin's kicked over his water bucket and doesn't have anything to drink."

"I . . . um . . . haven't had time to clean it up. I was just going to, but—" Ellie burst out.

"No more excuses," Mrs. Browning said firmly. "I think we have to accept that you're not ready to own a pony. You'd be better off going back to riding-school ponies for a while."

"No! I am ready. I know I am," Ellie insisted. "Please let me keep Turpin! I couldn't bear it if you sold him. I love him so much!"

"I know that, honey. No one's arguing about that," her mom said gently.

"Loving a pony isn't enough, I'm afraid," Ellie's dad added. "You have to accept the responsibility of taking care of one, too. I agree with your mom about this."

Steph chewed at her lip. Poor Ellie was getting a severe scolding. What could she do? She knew in her heart that Ellie had what it took to be a good pony owner. She could see that she loved Turpin almost as much as Steph loved Comet! Steph really wanted to help Ellie discover that for herself, but she might never get the chance to do that now.

On impulse, she stepped forward and
rushed straight into the stable.

The atmosphere inside was electric.

Ellie stood there facing her furious
parents with hunched shoulders. Her hands
were thrust into her jeans pockets. Tears
were trickling down her face.

Only Turpin was calm, placidly
pulling at his hay net with soft ripping and

chewing noises. The wobbly lines cut into his coat looked even worse in the sunshine pouring in through an overhead window.

"Hi, Ellie," Steph said breezily. "I sharpened my clippers and found the spare blades. So I can finish with Turpin's clip—oh . . . er . . . hi," she said. She looked around with wide eyes at Ellie's parents, as if she'd only just noticed that there was something wrong.

"Steph?" Mrs. Browning frowned. "*You* clipped Turpin?"

Steph nodded. "Um . . . yeah. I made a bit of a mess, didn't I? Sorry. I was hoping to clean him up before you saw him." She gave what she hoped was a convincingly guilty shrug.

Ellie's dad raised his eyebrows as he

turned to his daughter. "Ellie? Why didn't you tell us this?"

Ellie opened and closed her mouth. She wiped her wet eyes with the back of her hands as she threw a puzzled glance at Steph.

Steph took a deep breath and plunged in. "She probably didn't want to get me into trouble. Ellie didn't want me to clip Turpin, but I did it anyway. I s'pose I was showing off," she lied. "And then it all went wrong because my clippers were blunt."

"Well, at least you're honest," Mrs. Browning said tersely. "But it was a very irresponsible thing to do."

"I know. And I am really sorry," Steph repeated. She hung her head, not caring how much hot water she got into if it was going to help Ellie keep Turpin. "Especially since I knew Ellie would be in a lot of trouble if you saw Turpin looking so awful—even if it wasn't her fault." She had a sudden idea. "So that's why I've promised to . . . give Ellie a hand with mucking out and stuff."

Ellie was stunned. "Um . . . you have?"

Steph gave her a level look, pleading with her eyes for Ellie to go along with this. "Definitely. Remember? We agreed that I'd come over every day and help you get into a good routine with Turpin. I'm going to show you how to groom him, too, and pick out his hooves, aren't I?"

Ellie blinked at her, catching on at last. "That's right. We . . . um . . . only just arranged it. I haven't had time to tell you yet," she said to her parents.

Mr. Browning ran his hand through his hair. He grinned drily. "Well, I guess your mom and I didn't give you much of a chance to speak up. We did kind of barge right in. Maybe we were a bit hasty to talk about selling Turpin. What do you think?" he asked, looking at his wife.

"I think we should give Ellie another chance to show us that she's ready to be a responsible pony owner," Mrs. Browning said.

"Yay!" Ellie threw herself at her mom and dad, but not before giving Steph the biggest grin ever. "I won't disappoint you—or Turpin!" she promised.

Steph could tell that Ellie meant every word.

"Phew! Finished at last." Steph brushed back a strand of damp hair from her forehead.

Turpin looked amazing with his new clip. Steph's fingertips still tingled faintly, but that faded as the last few violet sparkles floating around the clippers blinked out.

"Wow! He looks *fab-u-lous*! You're the best!" Ellie exclaimed. "I promise not to try anything like that ever again without mentioning it to you first!"

The two girls grinned at each other. Steph felt happy that they seemed to be becoming such good friends.

Steph gazed adoringly at Comet, who was snuffling around in the empty stall. She couldn't have done the clip without him. He was her own wonderful secret,

never to be shared with anyone else.

"And thanks for what you said to Mom and Dad. It really worked," Ellie went on. "You didn't have to go as far as promising to come here every single day."

"Just you try to keep me away!" Steph said. "Besides, my parents are going to save up to get me a new pony so, in the meantime, I've got lots of spare time."

"Well, all right. But only if you agree to ride Turpin as much as you want."

Steph's grin stretched from ear to ear. "I was hoping you'd say that!"

Ellie gave her a big hug. "There's one thing confusing me. How come you got back here so quickly earlier? I'd barely returned from the woods when you arrived."

"Oh, that. Speedy's my middle name," Steph joked. *You'd never believe me if I told you!*

Ellie linked arms with her. "Let's go into the house. Mom can make us cold drinks."

Steph was about to agree when, suddenly, she heard a sound she'd been both hoping for and dreading: the hollow thud of galloping hooves overhead.

She stiffened. Destiny! There was no mistake.

As Comet raced out of the stable, Steph pulled away from a puzzled-looking Ellie and dashed after him. "There's something I have to do. I'll follow you into the house," she said.

Just as Steph reached the paddock, a twinkling rainbow mist drifted down around her. In the center of it, Comet stood there as his true self, a black-and-white pony no longer. Bright sunlight glowed on his noble arched neck, magnificent golden wings, and cream coat. His flowing mane and tail glistened like strands of the finest gold thread.

"Comet!" Steph gasped. She had almost forgotten how beautiful he was. "Do you have to leave right now?"

Comet's deep-violet eyes softened

with affection. "I must. If I am to catch Destiny and save her from our enemies."

Steph's throat ached with sadness as she knew she would have to be strong. She ran forward and threw her arms around Comet's shining neck. Laying her cheek against his silken warmth, she murmured adoringly, "I'll never forget you."

"I will never forget you either, Steph," he whinnied softly. He allowed her to hug

him one last time, then gently moved away. "Farewell, Steph. You have been a good friend. Ride well and true," he said in a deep, musical voice.

There was a final flash of violet light and a silent explosion of rainbow glitter that sprinkled around Steph and tinkled softly as it fell to the ground. Comet spread his wings and soared upward. He faded and was gone.

Steph blinked away tears, unable to believe that everything had happened so fast. Something lay on the grass. It was a single glittering gold wing feather. Bending down, she picked it up.

It tingled against her palm as it faded to a cream color. Steph slipped it into her pocket. She would always keep the feather to remind her of the wonderful adventure she and Comet had shared.

As she walked out of the paddock and around to the stable, Ellie appeared at the kitchen door, holding two glasses of orange juice.

A smile broke out on Steph's face as she went toward her. The rest of the summer vacation stretched ahead of her. She felt her spirits rise at the thought of countless days of shared fun with Ellie and Turpin.

"Take care, Comet. Thank you for being my friend. I hope you find Destiny and live happily together on Rainbow Mist Island," she whispered softly.

About the
AUTHOR

Sue Bentley's books for children often
include animals, fairies, and wildlife.
She lives in Northampton, England, and
enjoys reading, going to the movies, and
watching the birds on the feeders outside
her window. She loves horses, which she
thinks are all completely magical. One of
her favorite books is *Black Beauty*, which
she must have read at least ten times. At
school she was always getting scolded for
daydreaming, but she now knows that she
was storing up ideas for when she became
a writer. Sue has met and owned many
animals, but the wild creatures in her life
hold a special place in her heart.

Magic Ponies

Don't miss these
Magic Ponies books!

Don't miss these
Magic Kitten books!